# Hairy Dawg's Journey Through The Peach State

## Vince Dooley

### Illustrated by Josh Mirman

www.mascotbooks.com

Hairy Dawg was enjoying a relaxing summer on the campus of the University of Georgia. With football season fast approaching, Hairy Dawg decided to take one last summer vacation. He thought it would be great fun to take a journey throughout the Peach State, where he could see many interesting places and make new friends along the way.

Before hitting the road, Hairy Dawg stopped at the historic Arch and the Bulldog Statue on UGA's campus. "Goodbye, Hairy Dawg! Have a nice trip!" said a couple of his fans. The mascot packed his bags, hopped into the Hairy Dawg Mobile, and was on his way!

After leaving campus, Hairy Dawg explored the City of Athens. Outside City Hall, Hairy Dawg ran into a couple of Bulldog fans. The fans were happy to see their favorite mascot and called, "Hello, Hairy Dawg!"

Athens, Georgia is the proud home of the University of Georgia.

*Several famous music groups
call Athens home, including
R.E.M. and The B-52's.*

Knowing that Athens is famous for its music
scene, Hairy Dawg grabbed his guitar and joined
a band on stage. Hairy Dawg amazed the crowd
with his talent. The crowd roared in approval and
yelled, "Rock on, Hairy Dawg!"

*The Chattahoochee River runs from the mountains of Northeast Georgia to the southwestern part of the state.*

Hairy Dawg was ready to explore Georgia's natural wonders. His first stop outside Athens was the Chattahoochee River, where he went tubing with friends. Along the way, Georgia fans cheered, "How 'bout them Dawgs!"

After tubing, Hairy Dawg tried his hand at bass fishing. He reeled in an amazing catch! The fish said in a worried voice, "Hello, Hairy Dawg!"

Helen, Georgia is a replica of a Bavarian alpine village that hosts festivals throughout the year, attracting thousands of visitors annually.

Hairy Dawg's next stop was Helen, Georgia. Wanting to fit in, Hairy Dawg dressed in his best Bavarian attire and participated in a traditional dance. Hairy Dawg's new friends were amazed by his dancing skills. They shouted, "Bravo, Hairy Dawg!"

From Helen, Hairy Dawg made the short trip to Lake Burton in Northeast Georgia. Hairy Dawg hopped on water skis and glided over the water. Spectators called, "Go, Hairy Dawg, go!"

Hairy Dawg drove south to Atlanta, the capital of the Peach State. In Atlanta, there was so much for Hairy Dawg to do and see – he didn't know where to begin!

He had heard about the Georgia Aquarium, so he stopped there first. Inside, the mascot dressed in scuba gear and dove into the shark tank. Fortunately, the sharks were Georgia fans! The sharks chomped, "Hello, Hairy Dawg!"

The mascot traveled all over Atlanta on the MARTA, stopping next at Centennial Olympic Park. Hairy Dawg snapped a picture of Bulldog fans near the fountains. The fans grinned and said, "Cheeeeese, Hairy Dawg!"

*Centennial Olympic Park, with its "Fountain of Rings," opened in 1996 for the Atlanta Olympics and was a popular destination for pin traders during that year's Games.*

At an Atlanta-area amusement park, Hairy Dawg
rode roller coasters all day long. "Go, Hairy Dawg,
go!" cheered his friends.

Next, it was on to the Atlanta Zoo, where the
mascot was eager to see the famous panda bears.
The bears growled, "Hello, Hairy Dawg!"

At Stone Mountain, Hairy Dawg rode the gondola up to the top of the mountain. He was amazed at the mountain's size! Of course, he ran into more UGA fans there. The fans hollered, "How 'bout them Dawgs!"

The Confederate Memorial Carving on Stone Mountain features Jefferson Davis, Robert E. Lee, and Stonewall Jackson.

Over 125,000 race fans pack into Atlanta Motor Speedway on race days.

Hairy Dawg was ready to speed things up, so he stopped at Atlanta Motor Speedway. He drove the Hairy Dawg Mobile right onto the track, not knowing there was a race going on! The mascot placed the "pedal to the metal" and drove as fast as he could. Race fans cheered, "Go, Hairy Dawg, go!"

After a couple of laps, he parked his car and made his way to pit row. The crew chief was happy to get the mascot's help. He said to Hairy Dawg, "Thanks, good buddy!"

Hairy Dawg loved learning about famous Georgians, so he was off to the Georgia Sports Hall of Fame and the Georgia Music Hall of Fame, both in Macon. At the Sports Hall of Fame, he ran into many Georgia Bulldog fans. A little boy was thrilled to see his favorite mascot. He said, "Look, Dad, it's Hairy Dawg!"

At the Georgia Music Hall of Fame, Hairy Dawg learned about his favorite musicians. Outside, a couple said, "Hello, Hairy Dawg," but the mascot could not hear them because he was listening to his favorite song on his iPod.

In Macon, Hairy Dawg took a trolley tour. Macon residents cheered, "Hello, Hairy Dawg!"

Located in the center of the state, Macon, Georgia is known as the "Heart of Georgia."

As Hairy Dawg continued driving, he came across a peach orchard. Living in the Peach State, he loved peaches! He picked the juiciest peaches off a tree and gobbled them up. At a nearby peanut farm, he stopped to pick up a fresh jar of peanut butter. Yummy!

As he continued through Georgia's agriculture region, he came across a cotton farm. Hairy Dawg helped a farmer harvest cotton. The farmer said, "Thanks, Hairy Dawg!"

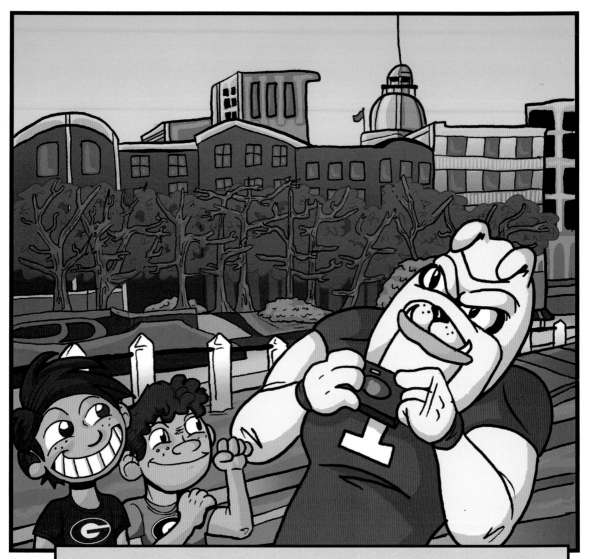

*Savannah was established in 1733 as the original capital of the colony and state of Georgia. Savannah is the hometown of the world's most famous bulldog mascot, Uga.*

Hairy Dawg continued to Savannah, Georgia, where he ran into tourists from all over the world. In historic downtown Savannah, the mascot took a picture of two of his young fans. The kids said, "Go, Bulldogs!"

On Jekyll Island, Hairy Dawg helped a young girl build a beautiful sandcastle. At the Georgia Sea Turtle Center, Hairy Dawg learned all about these amazing creatures. One little turtle swam right up to the mascot and snapped, "Go, Dawgs!"

Hairy Dawg was looking forward to driving up to Augusta, Georgia for the world's most famous golf tournament. At the golf course, he followed his favorite golfer for eighteen holes. The golfer took a mighty swing, turned to the mascot, and said, "How 'bout that drive, Hairy Dawg!"

*Augusta is Georgia's second largest city and is best known for hosting the golf tournament known as The Masters.*

Wanting to improve his own game, Hairy Dawg dressed in his best golf clothes and hit the links! He enjoyed playing golf, but he enjoyed driving the golf cart even more!

Finally, Hairy Dawg made it back to Athens, Georgia and the campus of the University of Georgia. As he lay in bed, he took a moment to think about all the places he visited and the many Georgia Bulldog fans he had met along the way.

As Hairy Dawg drifted off to sleep, he thought about how lucky he was to be the mascot at the University of Georgia.

Good night, Hairy Dawg!

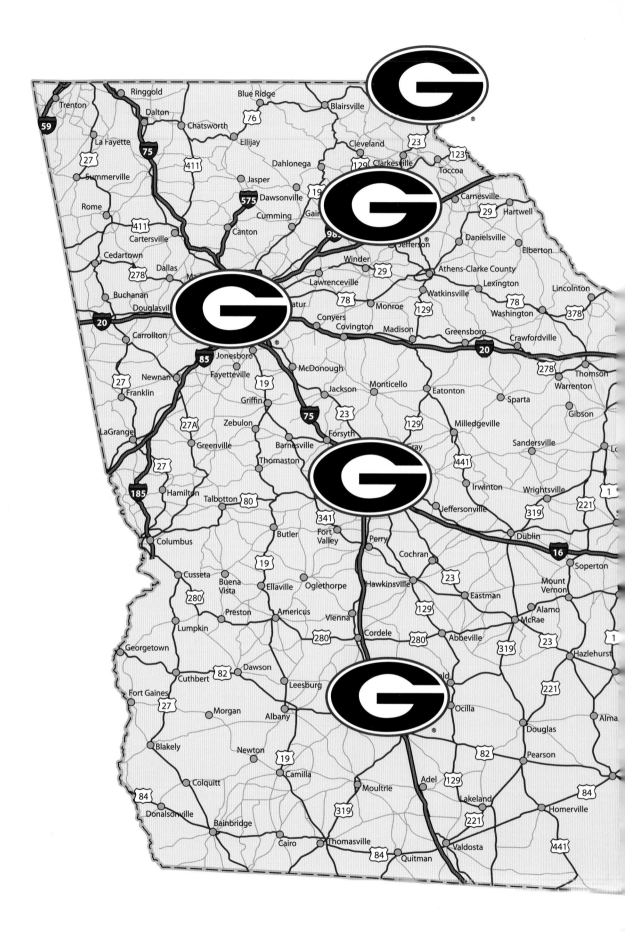

# Hairy Dawg's
## Journey Through
# The Peach State

For Georgia fans, young and old, especially my
grandchildren: Patrick, Catherine, Christopher, Ty, Joe,
Cal, Michael, Matthew, John Taylor, Peyton, and Julie Ann,
and their grandmother, Honey. ~ Vince Dooley

For more information about our products,
please visit us online at www.mascotbooks.com.

For more information, please contact Mascot Books,
P.O. Box 220157, Chantilly, VA 20153-0157

ISBN: 978-1-934878-21-7

Printed in the United States.

www.mascotbooks.com

# Title List

## Baseball

| | | |
|---|---|---|
| Boston Red Sox | Hello, *Wally*! | Jerry Remy |
| Boston Red Sox | *Wally The Green Monster And His Journey Through Red Sox Nation*! | Jerry Remy |
| Boston Red Sox | Coast to Coast with *Wally The Green Monster* | Jerry Remy |
| Boston Red Sox | A Season with *Wally The Green Monster* | Jerry Remy |
| Colorado Rockies | Hello, *Dinger*! | Aimee Aryal |
| Detroit Tigers | Hello, *Paws*! | Aimee Aryal |
| New York Yankees | Let's Go, *Yankees*! | Yogi Berra |
| New York Yankees | *Yankees* Town | Aimee Aryal |
| New York Mets | Hello, *Mr. Met*! | Rusty Staub |
| New York Mets | *Mr. Met* and his Journey Through the Big Apple | Aimee Aryal |
| St. Louis Cardinals | Hello, *Fredbird*! | Ozzie Smith |
| Philadelphia Phillies | Hello, *Phillie Phanatic*! | Aimee Aryal |
| Chicago Cubs | Let's Go, *Cubs*! | Aimee Aryal |
| Chicago White Sox | Let's Go, *White Sox*! | Aimee Aryal |
| Cleveland Indians | Hello, *Slider*! | Bob Feller |
| Seattle Mariners | Hello, *Mariner Moose*! | Aimee Aryal |
| Washington Nationals | Hello, *Screech*! | Aimee Aryal |
| Milwaukee Brewers | Hello, *Bernie Brewer*! | Aimee Aryal |

## College

| | | |
|---|---|---|
| Alabama | Hello, Big Al! | Aimee Aryal |
| Alabama | Roll Tide! | Ken Stabler |
| Alabama | Big Al's Journey Through the Yellowhammer State | Aimee Aryal |
| Arizona | Hello, Wilbur! | Lute Olson |
| Arkansas | Hello, Big Red! | Aimee Aryal |
| Arkansas | Big Red's Journey Through the Razorback State | Aimee Aryal |
| Auburn | Hello, Aubie! | Aimee Aryal |
| Auburn | War Eagle! | Pat Dye |
| Auburn | Aubie's Journey Through the Yellowhammer State | Aimee Aryal |
| Boston College | Hello, Baldwin! | Aimee Aryal |
| Brigham Young | Hello, Cosmo! | LaVell Edwards |
| Cal - Berkeley | Hello, Oski! | Aimee Aryal |
| Clemson | Hello, Tiger! | Aimee Aryal |
| Clemson | Tiger's Journey Through the Palmetto State | Aimee Aryal |
| Colorado | Hello, Ralphie! | Aimee Aryal |
| Connecticut | Hello, Jonathan! | Aimee Aryal |
| Duke | Hello, Blue Devil! | Aimee Aryal |
| Florida | Hello, Albert! | Aimee Aryal |
| Florida | Albert's Journey Through the Sunshine State | Aimee Aryal |
| Florida State | Let's Go, 'Noles! | Aimee Aryal |
| Georgia | Hello, Hairy Dawg! | Aimee Aryal |
| Georgia | How 'Bout Them Dawgs! | Vince Dooley |
| Georgia | Hairy Dawg's Journey Through the Peach State | Vince Dooley |
| Georgia Tech | Hello, Buzz! | Aimee Aryal |
| Gonzaga | Spike, The Gonzaga Bulldog | Mike Pringle |
| Illinois | Let's Go, Illini! | Aimee Aryal |
| Indiana | Let's Go, Hoosiers! | Aimee Aryal |
| Iowa | Hello, Herky! | Aimee Aryal |
| Iowa | Hello, Cy! | Amy DeLashmutt |
| Iowa State | Hello, Duke Dog! | Aimee Aryal |
| James Madison | Hello, Duke Dog! | Aimee Aryal |
| Kansas | Hello, Big Jay! | Aimee Aryal |
| Kansas State | Hello, Willie! | Dan Walter |
| Kentucky | Hello, Wildcat! | Aimee Aryal |
| LSU | Hello, Mike! | Aimee Aryal |
| LSU | Mike's Journey Through the Bayou State | Aimee Aryal |
| Maryland | Hello, Testudo! | Aimee Aryal |
| Michigan | Let's Go, Blue! | Aimee Aryal |
| Michigan State | Hello, Sparty! | Aimee Aryal |
| Minnesota | Hello, Goldy! | Aimee Aryal |
| Mississippi | Hello, Colonel Rebel! | Aimee Aryal |

## Pro Football

| | | |
|---|---|---|
| Carolina Panthers | Let's Go, Panthers! | Aimee Aryal |
| Chicago Bears | Let's Go, Bears! | Aimee Aryal |
| Dallas Cowboys | How 'Bout Them Cowboys! | Aimee Aryal |
| Green Bay Packers | Go, Pack, Go! | Aimee Aryal |
| Kansas City Chiefs | Let's Go, Chiefs! | Aimee Aryal |
| Minnesota Vikings | Let's Go, Vikings! | Aimee Aryal |
| New York Giants | Let's Go, Giants! | Aimee Aryal |
| New York Jets | J-E-T-S! Jets, Jets, Jets! | Aimee Aryal |
| New England Patriots | Let's Go, Patriots! | Aimee Aryal |
| Pittsburg Steelers | Here We Go, Steelers! | Aimee Aryal |
| Seattle Seahawks | Let's Go, Seahawks! | Aimee Aryal |
| Washington Redskins | Hail To The Redskins! | Aimee Aryal |

## Basketball

| | | |
|---|---|---|
| Dallas Mavericks | Let's Go, Mavs! | Mark Cuban |
| Boston Celtics | Let's Go, Celtics! | Aimee Aryal |

## Other

| | | |
|---|---|---|
| Kentucky Derby | White Diamond Runs For The Roses | Aimee Aryal |
| Marine Corps Marathon | Run, Miles, Run! | Aimee Aryal |
| Mississippi State | Hello, Bully! | Aimee Aryal |
| Missouri | Hello, Truman! | Todd Donoho |
| Nebraska | Hello, Herbie Husker! | Aimee Aryal |
| North Carolina | Hello, Rameses! | Aimee Aryal |
| North Carolina | Rameses' Journey Through the Tar Heel State | Aimee Aryal |
| North Carolina St. | Hello, Mr. Wuf! | Aimee Aryal |
| North Carolina St. | Mr. Wuf's Journey Through North Carolina | Aimee Aryal |
| Notre Dame | Let's Go, Irish! | Aimee Aryal |
| Ohio State | Hello, Brutus! | Aimee Aryal |
| Ohio State | Brutus' Journey | Aimee Aryal |
| Oklahoma | Let's Go, Sooners! | Aimee Aryal |
| Oklahoma State | Hello, Pistol Pete! | Aimee Aryal |
| Oregon | Go Ducks! | Aimee Aryal |
| Oregon State | Hello, Benny the Beaver! | Aimee Aryal |
| Penn State | Hello, Nittany Lion! | Aimee Aryal |
| Penn State | We Are Penn State! | Joe Paterno |
| Purdue | Hello, Purdue Pete! | Aimee Aryal |
| Rutgers | Hello, Scarlet Knight! | Aimee Aryal |
| South Carolina | Hello, Cocky! | Aimee Aryal |
| South Carolina | Cocky's Journey Through the Palmetto State | Aimee Aryal |
| So. California | Hello, Tommy Trojan! | Aimee Aryal |
| Syracuse | Hello, Otto! | Aimee Aryal |
| Tennessee | Hello, Smokey! | Aimee Aryal |
| Tennessee | Smokey's Journey Through the Volunteer State | Aimee Aryal |
| Texas | Hello, Hook 'Em! | Aimee Aryal |
| Texas | Hook 'Em's Journey Through the Lone Star State | Aimee Aryal |
| Texas A & M | Howdy, Reveille! | Aimee Aryal |
| Texas A & M | Reveille's Journey Through the Lone Star State | Aimee Aryal |
| Texas Tech | Hello, Masked Rider! | Aimee Aryal |
| UCLA | Hello, Joe Bruin! | Aimee Aryal |
| Virginia | Hello, CavMan! | Aimee Aryal |
| Virginia Tech | Hello, Hokie Bird! | Aimee Aryal |
| Virginia Tech | Yea, It's Hokie Game Day! | Frank Beamer |
| Virginia Tech | Hokie Bird's Journey Through Virginia | Aimee Aryal |
| Wake Forest | Hello, Demon Deacon! | Aimee Aryal |
| Washington | Hello, Harry the Husky! | Aimee Aryal |
| Washington State | Hello, Butch! | Aimee Aryal |
| West Virginia | Hello, Mountaineer! | Aimee Aryal |
| Wisconsin | Hello, Bucky! | Aimee Aryal |
| Wisconsin | Bucky's Journey Through the Badger State | Aimee Aryal |

Order online at **mascotbooks.com** using promo code " free" to receive **FREE SHIPPING!**

More great titles coming soon!

info@mascotbooks.com

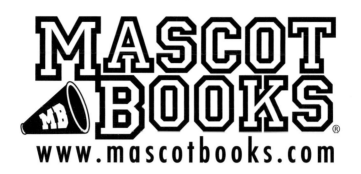
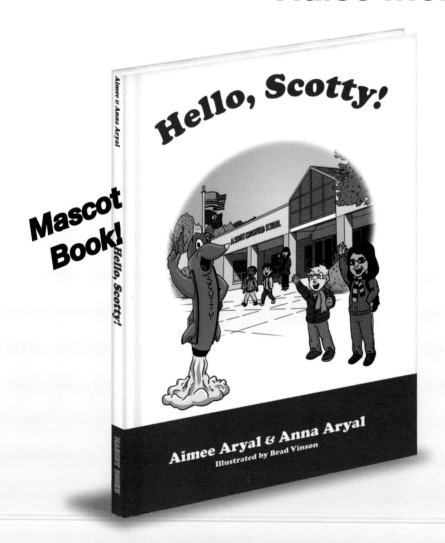

# Let Mascot Books create a customized children's book for your school or team!

## Here's how our fundraisers work ...

- Mascot Books creates a customized children's book with content specific to your school. When parents buy your school's book, your organization earns cash!

- When parents buy any of Mascot Books' college or professional team books, your organization earns more cash!

- We also offer options for a customized plush, apparel, and even mascot costumes!

**Mascot Costumes!**

Dougie the Dragon

**Mascot T-Shirts!**

Vinny the Duck

**Mascot Plush!**

Lulu the Ladybug

**For more information about the most innovative fundraiser on the market, contact us at info@mascotbooks.com.**